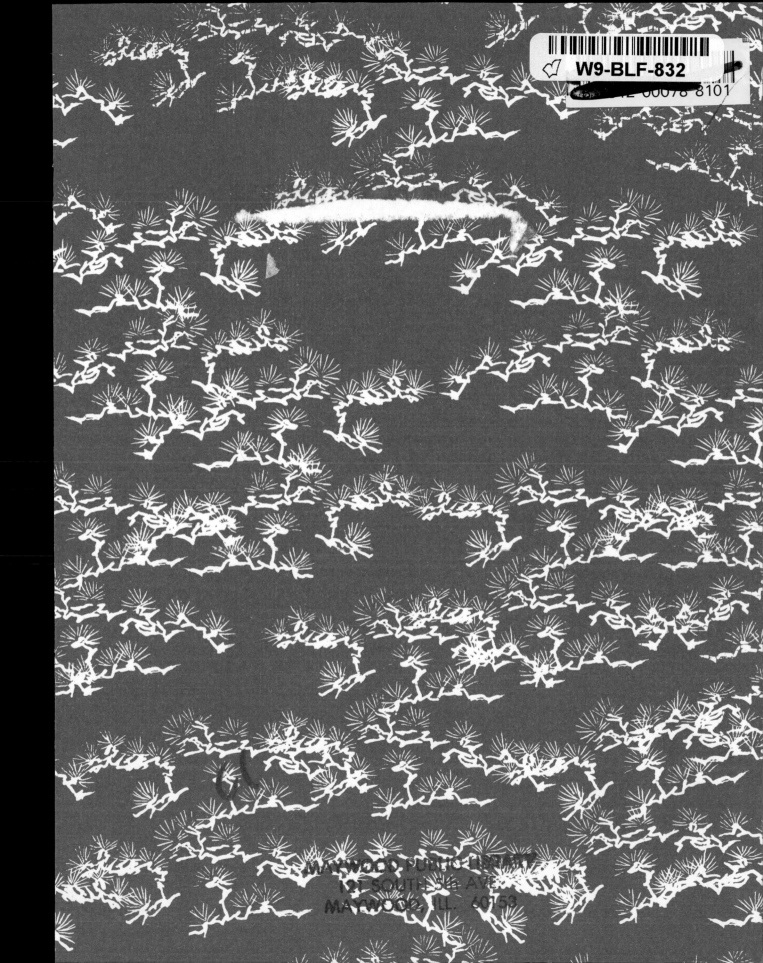

The Miracle Tree

The Miracle Tree

Christobel Mattingley

illustrated by
Marianne Yamaguchi

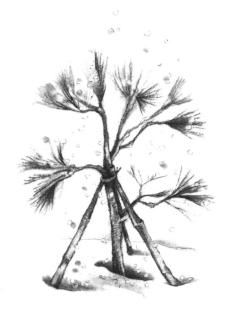

GULLIVER BOOKS
HARCOURT BRACE JOVANOVICH
San Diego   Austin   Orlando

First published in Australia by Hodder and Stoughton (Australia) Pty Limited
Text copyright © 1985 by Christobel Mattingley
Illustrations copyright © 1985 by Marianne Yamaguchi

Library of Congress Cataloging-in-Publication Data

Mattingley, Christobel.
  The miracle tree.

  "Gulliver books."
  Summary: Separated by the explosion of the atomic bomb, a husband, wife,
and mother carry on with their lives in the ruins of Nagasaki and are
eventually reunited one Christmas by a very special tree.
  [1. Nagasaki-shi (Japan)–History–Bombardment, 1945–Fiction.
2. Christmas–Fiction. 3. Trees–Fiction]
I. Yamaguchi, Marianne, ill. II. Title.
PZ7.M43543Mi 1986   [Fic]   86-45416
ISBN 0-15-200530-7

Printed by Everbest Printing Co, Hong Kong.

First edition

A B C D E

*For all who have suffered from Nagasaki and Hiroshima
and for all who work for peace.*

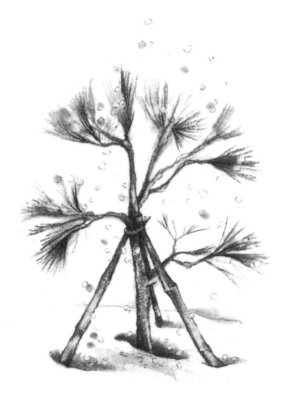

In the city of Nagasaki on the Japanese island of Kyushu three people lived for twenty years hoping for a miracle.

Taro was a gardener. As a young man he had gone to the war, leaving behind his new bride. Her skin was as smooth as a camellia petal, her hair was as shiny as a crow's wing, her eyes sparkled like pools in the sun, and her voice was as sweet as a nightingale's.

The thought of her beauty kept Taro's spirit alive all through the dark days and nights of fear and fighting, chaos and killing. And when at last the war ended, Taro decided that he would never kill or destroy again. He wanted only to live in peace with his beautiful wife and to create beauty by growing plants.

But when Taro returned to Japan, he learned that his wife had been sent to work in Nagasaki during the war. And an atom bomb had been dropped on Nagasaki.

He hurried there to look for her. But when he reached the city, he found that street after street lay waste. Hundreds and hundreds of houses up the hillsides lay in heaps of rubble. And nothing was left of the factory where his wife had worked except some twisted steel.

He went to the hospitals, hoping to find her. "Is my wife, Hanako Matsuda, here?"

The answer was always, "No. We have no patient of that name."

So Taro would describe her. "She is very beautiful. Her skin is like a camellia petal, her hair shines like a crow's wing, and her eyes are like pools in the sun."

Then the statement came, again and again, which chilled his heart. "No one is beautiful who has suffered atomic blast."

He joined one of the gangs clearing the shattered streets, the broken buildings, the crushed cars. They found plates and bottles where people had been eating and drinking, tools where people had been working, spectacles where people had been reading, even a clock that had stopped at two minutes past eleven when the bomb exploded.

They found skeletons of horses and sometimes human bodies. But never one that looked like Hanako. Taro's heart was broken, like the myriad pieces of broken lives he loaded each day into baskets to be cleared away. And his hands, raw from the roughness of the rubble, longed for the smoothness of leaves and the softness of soil.

The gangs worked for weeks. They worked

for months. They worked and worked. And Taro went many times to the hospitals. He asked everyone he met. But he did not find Hanako.

As the rubble was cleared, new buildings began to rise. But all was bare. There was not a leaf, not a flower, not a tree to be seen. Taro longed to bring beauty back to the stark streets.

He went to work for an old gardener who taught him the secrets of seeds and roots, leaves and shoots, and all he knew from a lifetime of planting and pruning, clipping, shaping, and trimming.

When the old man became too frail to tend the gardens he had cared for so long, Taro took over. Riding his bicycle, with his tools slung in a sack on his back, he visited houses all over the city. And everywhere he went he asked about his wife. But no one ever knew anything about her.

Taro tended all sorts of trees—persimmons, maples, cedars and cypresses, oaks and hollies, spruces, camellias, and pines of all sizes. And he loved every one of them. But his favorite tree of all was a pine he had planted himself, in a corner of the garden of a new house in one of the steep streets he had helped to clear.

It was a tiny pine, but already it promised

strength and beauty. Its needles were as smooth as a camellia petal, with a sheen like a crow's wing. But it was silent unless the wind blew, and then its voice was only the merest whisper.

Taro remembered the very day he had planted it. It was Christmas Day. He had heard the carols coming from a radio in a block of flats across the road. And as he worked, a string of people climbed up the narrow steps on their way to worship. The church, once a landmark, had been flattened by the bomb, but people still came to pray where it had been.

Taro had been too busy planting the tree to ask any of the people about his wife. But he remembered one woman, rather bent, carrying a string of paper cranes, who had stopped to bow to him and wish the tree well.

Taro visited the little tree twice a year to check its health and train its growth. The tree felt the love in his hands, and it grew well, strong, and shapely. Taro was proud of it. It was like his child.

The woman with the bent back, who saw the tree being planted, watched it grow also. She had come to Nagasaki at the end of the war, hoping to find her daughter. The sight of the city had shocked her, and she had joined a gang helping to clear the ruins. She had asked everyone she met, "Have you seen my daughter, my Hanako, my precious little flower?" But there was not a flower to be seen on those barren slopes, no trace of her daughter anywhere.

When the last ruins were cleared away, the woman stayed on. She was still looking, still hoping to find her daughter, who had left home at the beginning of the war to work in the city. With searing pain she remembered the day the letter had come. Her daughter wrote that she had met a man she loved. She asked her mother's pardon for having married him. He was a soldier going to war, and there had not been time enough to seek permission first.

The mother remembered the anger that had flared in her heart. Anger at the man who had taken her treasure. Anger at the disobedient daughter who had defied the marriage custom and gone her own way. She had burnt the letter, and the name of the man who had plucked her flower had crumbled into black ashes. And the letters that came afterward she burned without opening, the anger still smoldering in her heart.

Now she burned with remorse that she had not forgiven her daughter. She reproached herself that she had not written a blessing in reply. She was desolate that she could not remember the name of the man who had loved her daughter so much that he had taken her for his wife. But the name had vanished from her mind as the ashes from the letter had blown out of the window on that day long ago. And the bitterness in her heart was for her own actions.

She joined a group of people rebuilding the church and toiled every day lifting bricks, wheeling cement. And her back grew more bent, more bowed by her labor and by the load she carried in her heart. And her hair grew gray.

And although her hands were sore and bleeding,

night after night she folded paper cranes, tens upon tens, into strings of one hundred, looped together to make a thousand. A thousand paper cranes for the well-being of her daughter. And morning and evening as she went to and from her labors, the little tree was her comfort and joy. It was like a grandchild to her.

The tree brought hope to a third person also, who watched over it like a mother day and night from her room across the road. She had been sent to work in a factory in Nagasaki during the war. At first she was happy and proud to be serving her country, to be making bullets for her soldier husband to shoot at the enemy. And she sang as she worked.

Then she began to think of the wives in a far-off country who would never see their husbands again, of the children who would never see their fathers again, of the mothers who would never see their sons again, because of the bullets she was making. And she thought of those wives, her sisters in a far-off country, who were making bullets to kill her husband. Her heart grew cold with sadness, and she no longer sang, except for a low keening lullaby.

Then one day a bomb dropped that destroyed the

factory and most of her workmates. She survived, but her hair fell out, her skin was scarred and ridged from burns, and her eyes were dull and blank. When she saw her reflection in the mirror she did not know herself. When they asked her name, she said, "I am a withered leaf." And when they asked about her family, she said, "My husband was killed at the war. My mother is dead." Then she did not speak again. So they called her Shizuka.

When she left the hospital at last, a place was found for her in a new building near the church. For a long time she sat by the window of her room, without seeing or hearing anything. Then one day she saw the gardener come with a bundle on his bicycle. She saw him prepare the soil. She saw him unwrap the tree. She saw him unfold the straw from its roots. She watched him plant the tree.

She saw the woman with the bent back stop and bow. She looked at the string of paper cranes, pink, green, yellow, blue, orange, and red, like flowers in the gray street. She listened to the woman wishing the tree well and the gardener's reply. The sound of their voices echoed through her. And the ice in her heart and the numbness in her mind began to thaw.

That night, long after the gardener had packed his tools and ridden away and the woman with the bent back had returned to her home, she still sat by the window, looking down on the tree. When the first star rose bright

and clear over the place where the church had been, for
the first time in years feelings and words surged through
her.

Her fingers tingled as she picked up a pen and
began to write. Not a letter to her soldier husband. He
had been killed. Not a letter to her mother. She was
dead. But a poem. A poem about the tree.

In the weeks that followed she watched the tree. She watched it in the sunlight.

She watched it in the moonlight.

She watched it in the wind that blew up from the sea.

She watched it in the rain that swept down from the mountains. And she wrote poems about the sun and the moon, the wind and the rain.

Winter passed. Spring came. And the little tree thrived and grew. At mid-summer, six months after he had planted it, the gardener came back. The woman in the window watched him gently trim its buds and pluck its needles. The woman with the bent back passing on her daily way stopped to speak to him. She gathered the needles and wrapped them carefully like the first-cut locks of a child's hair and went on up the steps to her work. That night the woman in the window wrote another poem.

Summer passed. Autumn came. The tree flourished, and the woman in the window wrote more poems. About the sky, the clouds, and the birds—the brown forktail kites that soared and circled over the city, the black crows that cawed and settled on the rooftops, and the pigeons that spun in whirring wheels and sped like single arrows.

Christmas came with carols on the radio and people carrying presents as they walked along the street. No one brought a present to the woman in the window. But on Christmas Day the gardener visited the tree, and the woman with the bent back stopped to speak to him. And the woman in the window was not lonely, because it seemed as if they were her family. And she loved them. So she wrote another poem.

She began to love all the people passing in the street—the children playing and going to school, the women bringing home their shopping, the men going to work. And she wrote poems about skipping ropes and tops and paper kites that flew like birds, and about laughter, loyalty, duty, and love.

She watched the women hanging the bedding to air and pegging out the washing. She watched old people with brooms and buckets going to tend the tombs of their ancestors. She watched men in trucks delivering bundles of cabbages, bags of mandarins, baskets of fish. The tree grew, and so did her pile of poems.

Spring came with the green of hope on the trees in the Peace Park, and in autumn the hillside glowed with fulfillment. Flowers came back, in pots on window sills and in bunches in the hands of passersby. Again cats slept and stalked alone on roofs and ledges, and dogs walked with their masters in the street.

The years slipped by, marked by festivals like kites

on a string—New Year's Day and the Emperor's Birthday, when women dressed in their best kimonos, the kite-flying contest when teams of young men competed to fly their huge decorated kites, Boys' Day with cloth carp on bamboo poles, Okunchi with the procession of shrines and palanquins and dragons, the spring and autumn equinoxes, and many more.

The woman in the window watched them all, and her glimpses became poems. But the times she looked forward to most were not the festivals, but Christmas and mid-summer, for then the gardener came to tend the tree.

The tree had grown so big that Taro needed two days to prune it now. He had to give up some of his other trees to spend the extra time on the pine. And he had to bring ladders and poles in a trailer behind his bicycle. It was hard riding, but he did not begrudge it. The tree was worth it. Its beauty was as subtle as a silk painting, as haunting as a poem. It brought hope and happiness to everyone who saw it.

When the church was completed at last, its domes stood up against the sky and its bell rang joyfully across the city. As the woman in the window wrote a poem about it, she wondered if she would ever see the old woman again.

But the old woman continued to come past every day to visit the church. And she continued to make the strings of paper cranes that hung over her bent back like rainbows of hope. Her hair had gone white. She was so stooped and stiff she had to turn her head to look up at the tree she loved. She became slower and slower climbing the steps. But she still came.

The woman in the window wrote a poem about her. And another poem about the paper cranes. But it was becoming harder for her to hold her pen. She was growing weaker every day.

She longed to see the gardener just once more and to hear his voice. She counted the days until Christmas on her calendar and began to fold paper cranes, so that her wish might be fulfilled. She had no paper except for the sheets on which her poems were written. So she folded her poems of life and people, of every day and eternity, into paper cranes of hope.

Slowly, painfully, the strings of cranes grew longer and the piles of poems grew smaller. On Christmas Eve she folded the last crane. She tied the strings together. Then she picked up her pen again. There was still one poem she wanted to write. She wanted to thank the gardener for the tree.

She sat at the window all night, waiting for the dawn that would bring the gardener. Her heart grew light as he arrived. With joy she watched him walk around the tree, stroking its trunk, touching its branches. She watched him set up his ladder and unpack his pruning sheers, and as he began his labor of love, her heart began to sing.

Taro paused and looked around. He looked up into the tree and shook his head. He could have sworn he heard a nightingale. But no nightingale could be in such a city street, not even in this tree that was the joy of his life.

He continued to cut and shape, prune and pluck, with a strange sense of expectancy. He wondered if the old woman with the bent back would come as she always did. He looked forward to her praise and admiration of his beloved tree. It gladdened his heart to share his joy with her.

But she had aged, and her steps were slow and painful. Perhaps she could no longer make her pilgrimage. Taro felt a sudden pang that, in his concentration on the tree, he had never known her name. He reproached himself for his discourtesy and resolved that if she should come this once more, he would make up for his oversight of twenty years.

Just as the church bell began to ring, the old woman came. And even through the echoes of the bell Taro thought he heard the nightingale once more. He looked up into the tree and saw a small white shape like a star fluttering down.

He climbed his ladder and picked the star from its resting place on the topmost branch. He saw with surprise that it was a paper crane, and his hand tingled as it lay in his palm. He noticed writing on the folds and opened it carefully. He read the poem, and he looked up at the building across the street where the woman sat at the window.

"Come, Mother," Taro said respectfully to the old woman whose name he still did not know. He gave her a spray of the cut pine, as he had done twice a year for almost twenty years, and led her gently across the street.

Together they climbed the stairs, and Taro knocked on the door of a room whose nameplate said SHIZUKA.

The woman sitting by the window had skin as ridged as pine bark and hair as tufty as unplucked pine needles. Her voice as she bade them enter was as dry and thin as a rustle of paper. But her eyes, which were full of tears, sparkled like pools in the sun as she looked at the gardener and the woman with the bent back.

Taro felt as if a hundred thousand seeds were springing into blossom in his brain and a million leaves were unfolding all about him, cool and green and full of promise. He gazed with joy on the ravaged face before him and his voice rang like a glad bell as he said, "You are my Hanako!"

Hanako's tears ran down her scarred cheeks as she heard the response to the love that had sustained her for twenty years. "You are my Taro," she whispered in wonder. And turning to the old woman with the bent back, she said, "And you are my mother. I beg your pardon for marrying without permission. This is my husband, Taro Matsuda."

TARO MATSUDA. The old woman saw again her daughter's writing on the page as it scorched and curled above the flame. She looked at the man who had chosen her flower for his bride and who had given her the pine tree for her lonely years.

As Taro said, "I ask your forgiveness for the wrong I did," the old woman knew that her paper cranes had not been in vain. Her daughter's tears extinguished the embers of unhappiness in her heart, and she said, "You are both forgiven."

Hanako laid her cranes across her mother's shoulders. "Will you take them to church for me?"

Taro said, "You shall take them yourself. There is still time. We shall all go together."

And so after more than twenty years Hanako walked again in the street among people she loved. And as Taro helped his wife and her mother up the steps to the church, he blessed the tree for the miracle it had brought.

Hanako stood in the doorway of the church that her mother had helped to rebuild from rubble. Every column was hung with paper cranes as gay as the flowers on a bride's kimono. She looked at her own, so plain and white. They seemed out of place. There was no room for them.

Then she saw in a corner a baby lying on straw, with a sheep, an ox, and a donkey nearby. Her heart yearned for the baby she would never have. Her arms longed for the baby she would never hold. Into his outstretched empty hands she placed her cranes, patterned with pain and love, suffering and rejoicing.

And as she stood together for the first time with her husband and her mother, in her heart was the prayer that people everywhere feel on Christmas Day and every day, "Let peace prevail on earth."